SOUTH EAST MYSTERIES

Edited By Machaela Gavaghan

First published in Great Britain in 2018 by:

Young Writers
Remus House
Coltsfoot Drive
Peterborough
PE2 9BF
Telephone: 01733 890066
Website: www.youngwriters.co.uk

All Rights Reserved
Book Design by Spencer Hart
© Copyright Contributors 2018
SB ISBN 978-1-78896-986-4
Printed and bound in the UK by BookPrintingUK
Website: www.bookprintinguk.com
YB0381U

FOREWORD

Young Writers was created in 1991 with the express purpose of promoting and encouraging creative writing. Each competition we create is tailored to the relevant age group, hopefully giving each pupil the inspiration and incentive to create their own piece of work, whether it's a poem or a short story. We truly believe that seeing their work in print gives pupils a sense of achievement and pride in their work and themselves.

For Stranger Sagas, we challenged secondary school pupils to write a mini saga – a story in just 100 words. They were given the choice of eight story starters to give their imaginations a kick-start:

- Today, I hired someone to solve my murder...
- Don't go in the woods, they told me...
- I looked around, desperately searching for an escape...
- "Tell me everything you know, child..."
- My torch flickered and went out. I was alone in the darkness...
- I knew there would be consequences, but I did it anyway...
- *Please let this be a dream*, I thought...
- "You can save only one," the voice said...

They could use any one of these to begin their story, or alternatively they could choose to go it alone and create that all important first line themselves. With bizarre beginnings, mysterious middles and enigmatic endings, the resulting tales in this collection cover a range of genres and showcase the talent of the next generation. From fun to frightening to the weird and wonderful, these mini sagas are sure to keep you entertained and take you to strange new worlds.

CONTENTS

Newman Catholic College, Brent

THE MINI SAGAS

My Love Beside Me, My Honour Behind Me

I knew there would be consequences but I did it anyway. Haya, modest, I failed to keep the honour of my name. He seized my hand robustly, giving me tenacity. Thoughts invaded my brain, taking over the components and defeating me, welcoming dread, despair, dismay. "Abba, Ammi, Agha!" Running so swiftly, I could feel my kidneys drying out, throbbing from thirst. Conquering Neelam Bridge gave me a sudden hope but precipitously, I heard gunshots. My heart sank into my stomach, my body paralysed, my feet chained and as I revolved my head around, my love beside me, honour behind me.

Maliha Khan (14)
Copthall School, Mill Hill

Judgement Day!

"You can save only one," the voice said. The earth screamed. The timer began. One minute to decide. Who would I choose? The old, helpless lady? The vulnerable child? Or the innocent ones? Time was running out. The red, raging magma rose through the fractured ground. It was as if the devil had finally woken up. Lightning fired across the sky. The wind howled in the night. Screams, screeches and shrieks. Ten seconds left and my heart was sprinting. Time was a thief. My mind switched sides for a moment. Did I want to save anyone?

Zahra Bagrami (14)
Copthall School, Mill Hill

The Kidnapped

"Tell me everything you know, child. About the man you call your father," said the mysterious man.
"No!" screamed a young girl. *Bang!* The gun's bullet shot past her head. "Argh!" screamed the girl.
The man repeated, "Tell me everything you know and if you say no, tell me why."
"Because my dad's dead so if I could, I would," the young girl said calmly.
Bang!
"I have no use for you." The girl was shot in the head, her body hidden. Another bang. The man lay next to the girl he'd just killed.

Branden Holman-Morris (13)
Dover Grammar School For Boys, Dover

Just One

"You can only save one," the cursed spirit threatened. I glanced over at Henry, then to Helen.
"No, this isn't right. I did your dirty work for you!" I replied.
"Ah yes I know but if you won't choose either of them, then they shall both die!" the spirit croaked at me and I saw a weapon raised up on Henry.
"Alright! I choose both." I made a run for the weapon, broke my cuffs off and destroyed the cursed spherical demon. However, one life for another, I traded lives with the demon. I was cursed.
"Mike, you're cursed."

Oliver Huxley (12)
Dover Grammar School For Boys, Dover

The Tunnel Darkness

Ally and Noah slowly trudged towards a small concrete opening on a tiny hill. It was disguised by tall, emerald-green grass. Curiously, they shifted closer and closer like a falcon hunting its prey. Eventually, they entered the tunnel system that was wearing a blanket of graffiti. As they gazed up, they saw a massive spider with bright red, menacing eyes sat on a huge, dusty, golden cobweb. Looking into the darkness of the tunnels, they could see no end. They ventured deep into the tunnels when Ally's torch switched off. *Crack! Crunch!* There were heavy footsteps behind them...

Sam Elliott (13)
Dover Grammar School For Boys, Dover

The Last Light

The last flickering sparks hissed and my stomach churned. Scrabbling onto the nearest surface, I fled. This was the unknown. My dense, pounding breath broke the everlasting silence. Ahead, the ebony hinted to nothing. *Drip!* Grim liquid fell onto the floor. An abysmal crack ricocheted off of the enclosed tunnel that held me prisoner. Cluelessly, I clambered forwards, or backwards for that matter. My heart was raging the depths of hell. *Clunk!* The icy blow penetrated my legs as I smacked the bitter ground. A shadow emerged into the darkness. I knew, game over.

Harry Broom (12)
Dover Grammar School For Boys, Dover

An Unanswered Cry

"Tell me everything you know, child," he said. I never thought I'd be in a grim situation like this and I couldn't remember what stupid decisions put me in it, the choices that put me in the dark, mysterious cave, being asked mysterious questions by mysterious characters. I didn't know why I was put in the centre of an investigation about the questionable disappearance of my father. Deep down, I knew it wasn't my fault but my weak nature stopped me from denying their accusations, which were somewhat true. I answered, "Everything?"

Finlay Gaffney (12)
Dover Grammar School For Boys, Dover

The Butcher

I looked around, desperately searching for an escape. Heavy footsteps loudly approached me, my heart rate increased from 100 to 220 BPM. I froze, my mouth drier than the Sahara Desert. Goosebumps ran over my body, the footsteps became louder and a dark silhouette started to form in the darkness. I zoned back into reality and studied my surroundings. The walls were painted in dark red blood, the figure came into sight, holding a weapon of torture. The weapon cackled through the tunnel. I went cold. Suddenly, I heard a yell. The figure rushed forward, killing me instantly.

Yad Fazula (13)

Dover Grammar School For Boys, Dover

The Cursed Woods

Don't go into the woods, they told me. Of course, I didn't listen. I searched for the mysterious treasure of the cursed woods. Legends say it's protected by a horrifying beast with forty razor-sharp teeth and bright red eyes. It didn't stop me though. Nothing would. I walked around for a while and stumbled upon a tall tree with a rusty, metal door covered in claw marks. *Creepy.* I reluctantly opened the door and walked inside to find the mysterious treasure and the beast. Its eyes met mine as its mouth drooled uncontrollably, then it ate me.

Adam Fitchett (13)
Dover Grammar School For Boys, Dover

A Way Out

We looked around, desperately searching for an escape. Inside the house, we found two coat hangers swinging back and forth. I grabbed them and quickly pressed one against Leo's chest. Being afraid of heights, he was reluctant at first but with doses of persuasion, he gave in. I jumped swiftly. Loosening the wire, I carefully jumped down. Leo was close behind as the wire snapped in half. Alarms shook the prison, shots were fired in my direction but all I could think of was Leo. With a tight grasp onto the wire, with hesitation after pulling him up, we ran.

Aric Clarke Wood (15)
Dover Grammar School For Boys, Dover

The Room

My torch flickered and went out, a plague of darkness filled the room. The bitter air stabbed my back. I stood still, unable to move. The wind whispered in my ear, persuading me to move. I didn't dare. The piercing creak of the tattered door alerted me - I turned around. Blue eyes glared at me, glowing wildly in the empty darkness. My heart raced; I started to panic. What was this thing? Its malicious growl rumbled in a deep tone. Its spiny body twisted, spiralling like a helter-skelter. Its sharp, blade-like ears cut through the air. It attacked...

Elliot Betts (13)
Dover Grammar School For Boys, Dover

The Never-Ending Game

Left, right, left, right, left, *whack!* The crowd roared as the ball collided with the back of the net. The referee's whistle blew piercingly. "Goal!" John came up behind me and leapt on me, putting me to the floor. I hit my head...
I lifted my head with open eyes. I heard muffled screams and loud bangs repeatedly. Where was I? All I heard was white noise as men from young to old were having holes blown into their chests, causing an eruption of blood. Boats marooned onto the beach of Normandy, followed by half-dead men piling out.

William Hollobon (13)
Dover Grammar School For Boys, Dover

The Fire

"You can only save one," the voices said. The fire danced behind them. I prepared like a competitor before their event. Swiftly, I ran. They submerged me and choked me. There she was.

"Come on!" I screamed, now holding my breath, panicking. I scrambled to the window. Panting, I headed for the door, being buried by a cloud of smoke and ash. My house threw bricks and wood at me. My dog raced past me and jumped to everyone else outside. I slowed, tripping, falling, choking. I cried as the ash buried me in my grave. The noises faded...

Cody Chamberlain (12)

Dover Grammar School For Boys, Dover

Monsters

Blinding lights awoke me from my slumber. A girl and boy, both possibly seventeen, crouched beside me. I tried to get up. Yellow danced in my eyes as I clutched my head in agony. "Noir, ger ambrosia and nectar." Ambrosia and nectar? Before I could figure out what they could be, Noir came back with a strip of yellow gum and a flask. After I'd eaten and drank some of what was given to me, I was feeling as good as usual. Noir whispered, trembling, "Flare must be the guy, the son of Hecate." The walls shook wildly. "Monsters!"

Adam Dent (13)
Dover Grammar School For Boys, Dover

I Never Listen

Don't go into the woods, they told me. Don't go near the tree, they told me. Don't eat the blue mushroom, they told me. But I never listened. Looking in awe at the forest, the tree lured me in and I edged closer and closer, not knowing the consequences. Reaching out towards the glossy, blue mushroom, the first touch cursed me. It entered my body through my now-discoloured fingers. My head started to hurt. All of a sudden, my neck was itchy. Everything was hurting, my eyes sluggishly closed. I felt my consciousness slip away. What had I done?

Charlie Hixon (12)

Dover Grammar School For Boys, Dover

Only One

"You can only save one," the man said. He was dressed in a dark matte black tailored suit, paired with gloomy shades. It was either my mother or father, but I wanted neither. My mother was a Nazi officer, desperate for blood. My father enjoyed torturing my brothers and sisters. The man looked at me, pushing me for an answer. I looked around, desperately searching for an escape. However, it wasn't easy to leave Auschwitz with soldiers covering every inch of the facility so I had to make my choice. However, I could only save one of them...

Samuel Goodwin (15)
Dover Grammar School For Boys, Dover

No Escape!

I looked around, desperately searching for an escape. Trapped inside the mouth of Hell, trapped inside an insidious revenge, trapped inside Hell's nightmare. My fear made my body, as though ice had replaced my spine. A colossal image encased the corners as I ran for my life. The expectation of death awaited me. Peering out, a gloomy manor, not big but not small, entered my bloodshot eyes. Once again, I looked around to realise nothing was there. All of a sudden, a flash of light appeared in the sky to reveal all that was there. I was wrong...

Sebastian Hadley (12)
Dover Grammar School For Boys, Dover

Mysterious Car

I was nearly home when I was blinded by these beaming lights coming from ahead. The engine roared like a tiger. There was never anyone down this road. This shook me that someone was there. My heart was racing and sweat trickled down my face. The noisy piece of junk. Well, that's what it sounded like, still hadn't reached me with the road being a wreck. *Beep, beep* the car barked out, ringing in my ears. Now it was close to me and started slowing down. With squinted eyes, I examined the driver's seat. No one was to be seen...

Alex Keir (14)

Dover Grammar School For Boys, Dover

Flee The Facility

I gazed around, longing for something to hack. I could hear the beast's uncomforting heart beating. He was now near. I leapt through the shattered window, over the large oak dining table; there was a blue computer screen. This was the last one. I began to hack. My friend had escaped! Alex ran to come and help me. There was still time! The lights blew. Darkness. I could see the emitting light of the red crystal by the beast's hands. How could we get out? The glow of sinister green eyes impaled my shaking body. We lunged for an escape...

Jake Meager (13)

Dover Grammar School For Boys, Dover

Rudolph

The mischievous murderer was now on to me. My heart was pounding. Every second felt like an hour. I saw a pistol lying on the ground, covered in blood. Then I heard loud footsteps. *Boom! Boom!* Hiding was now my only option. Then again, *boom! Boom!* I heard music getting louder and louder. Rudolph the Red-Nosed Reindeer. I saw a kid going towards the man playing the music and then he was gobbled up in one! The music was carrying on relentlessly. He spotted me peeking through and started heading straight for me. Why me?

Ryan Whittall (11)
Dover Grammar School For Boys, Dover

Trench Escape

The gas funnelled through the trenches, their hands reaching for safety as if drowning in a sea of poison. The bombshells were all around, causing my ears to ring. They were screaming out for help but I couldn't hear their deafening screeches. My reactions kicked in and I ran in to save them. Scared and shocked, I stopped. My hands were shaking. My blood pumping, I sat there, confused and crying. *Who should I save?* I started to lose control of my body as I crawled out of the gas. I sat there in a ball as we all died.

William Dedman (13)
Dover Grammar School For Boys, Dover

Hunted

I desperately search for an escape, time running low as more beasts claw at the frail door that separates us. Then it is clear, my only exit is the delicate door, soon to be broken down by beasts anyway. I prepare to accept my defeat before spotting a pocket-sized, hidden window. As I desperately dash towards the modest glass pane, a large roar sounds as the door is broken down by beasts. In a desperate rush for time, I climb the stacked boxes but as a glimmer of hope is revealed, a rough hand clutches at my right leg...

James George (13)
Dover Grammar School For Boys, Dover

A Pirate's Tale

Waves as high as the mist crashed against the hall. Rain splashed down on my face as lightning flickered across the sky. The wood and ropes screamed as the huge tentacles rose, men ran to arms. The world slowed down, I could see the raindrops. The huge tentacles came down, splitting the beautiful ship in two. At one end, I could see Jack, a tall, nimble pirate. He summoned the storm, pinned down by a huge tentacle. A voice roared at me that I could only save one but my instincts told me to run. I snapped into action...

George Cullen (13)
Dover Grammar School For Boys, Dover

The Darkness In My Head

I was scared and frustrated at the edge of the bridge. I thought of all the heartless and senseless things everyone had said in the past months and years. *I can't take this anymore, please let it be a dream.* The words made the darkness in my head grow until it covered me fully to where I couldn't control my emotions or actions. I couldn't take it any longer. *Please let this be a dream.* I had been worried about what I would do under the darkness, so I was deciding whether to end it all...

Cameron Finnis (13)
Dover Grammar School For Boys, Dover

Soulless Androids

I looked around, desperately searching for an escape but death had caught me and I knew it. I had no choice, he forced me. With the realisation that death was on me, I knew they wouldn't have given me a second chance. They were going to kill me! I slumped onto the cold, metal floor of the lift and a voice comforted me. He was there again but I gave no reaction. He kept trying but I didn't care, the lift reached eighty-one and they were all there. I gave no reaction, they just did their job, soulless androids.

Luca Dean Romeo Chatterton (13)
Dover Grammar School For Boys, Dover

The Trenches

The guns fall silent, the wind stops howling. A good way to start 1916, in the trenches on the Western Front. We are all fed up of the trenches, it's wet, cold and demoralising. The end of the war seems impossible to reach, like a million miles away. Big plans are being made, the generals state. This is the year, they say. The year to win the war. Everyone in the trenches knows it isn't going to end. We all think the only way out is death. The big push is happening this year. See you soon, January 1st 1916.

Dan Smith (14)
Dover Grammar School For Boys, Dover

The Dark Woods

Please let this be a dream, I thought. It was dark. It was cold. It was wet in the woods. The trees were gently drifting to and fro. I had no idea what was about to happen. Then bugs started quickly scurrying back into their dens. Thundering along, I was being chased by a hooded man. It seemed to last for hours, then I tripped on a tall trunk. The man gained on me. I gave in. The footsteps became louder and started to shake the ground. I lay there, unable to move. *There is no escape,* I thought...

Fred Deveson (13)
Dover Grammar School For Boys, Dover

Bad Match

My torch flickered and then went out. (I was stupid.) I was in the basement because of my Tinder date, who appeared young but turned out to be the infamous Fred Bing-Bong, the man who had killed over thirty-two people! I stood at the mercy of him, scared, still and too worried to scream for help. I shouldn't have come to this hellish place, I was stupid to come alone! He paced around me, looking for the best place to start his torture. I cried for my life as he laughed like a maniac and looked at me evilly...

William Crickson (13)
Dover Grammar School For Boys, Dover

The Van

"Tell me everything you know, child!" demanded the man as I sat in his white van. His van was as long as a giraffe's neck. Inside, it was like a long tunnel. As I sat at the front of the loading bay, facing towards the back door, he was driving along, then came to a complete halt. I heard the car behind us screech as their tyres locked into place. I slid whilst trying to grip onto something. I hit the back doors of the van. My legs hit the van, leaving a dent more than fifty centimetres long...

Joe Morgan (13)
Dover Grammar School For Boys, Dover

The Shadow

It was dark. I climbed out of bed and walked downstairs. I grabbed a torch from the cupboard and snuck out the back door. Suddenly, I heard a hiss. I saw a small, black shadow run past me. Curious, I followed it round to the front of the house. It ran behind the car. Suddenly, my torch went out. Using only moonlight, I stalked towards the beast. I felt something brush against my leg. I looked down and saw that this was no dangerous beast, this was my cat, Shadow! I picked her up and carried her to my bed.

Braidan Stratton (12)
Dover Grammar School For Boys, Dover

Preserved

I looked around, desperately searching for an escape. I didn't know how I ended up there. This place seemed like an endless cave, only as time went on, it seemed to feel like home. Food was there and there were no soft drinks or alcohol, only one bottle, which I filled up every day by a faucet in the wall. This place wasn't a cave as such, more like an empty corridor with vegetation everywhere. It was like I was being preserved, contained, as if I was a trophy in a trophy case. Could this be true?

Keaton Bradberry (15)
Dover Grammar School For Boys, Dover

The Woods

They warned me about this bewitched hidden forest but I disobeyed them and the rules, as I usually do. A child's laugh comes from the woods to the left of me. The night partially blinds me but I can make out a silhouette of a house.
I arrive there and the rocking chair next to the door starts rocking. The door opens with a creak, notifying anyone inside. I hear the laugh again, this time from the main room. I go in and there is a seat in front of the TV and I fade into the eternal darkness...

Daniel Handy (13)
Dover Grammar School For Boys, Dover

The Head

The floorboards creaked, I snuck to the staircase. I stood fumbling in my bag to get my torch. Suddenly, *boom!* "Argh!" A high-pitched scream. Someone fell to the ground. I turned on my light and staggered up the stairs. A hand on the back of my neck, my head spun as quick as a bullet. No one there, I headed to a room. I looked at the closed door, wondered about opening it or just sprinting home. I stared at a decapitated head. It stared back at me. My torch flickered and went out...

Samuel Gough (13)
Dover Grammar School For Boys, Dover

Knocked Down

"I, uh, I, what?" was what I said before they did it. It was dark but colourful, black but white. Still but fast. I felt pains in my head. I wasn't in control. Noises were heard as if they were miles away. I was moving but all that was happening for me was stillness. My arms were now screaming and so were my legs. What was happening? The next thing I knew, I was inside a cage, dazed and exhausted. My head was painfully aching and my arms felt like they had been gnawed off. I was dying...

Jack Clayton (13)
Dover Grammar School For Boys, Dover

The Curious Cave

The cave stood barely a metre ahead of me. I knew if I went into the cave and people found out that there would be consequences but I went in anyway. As the overwhelming sense of curiosity crept into my body, I entered the cave and slowly made my way deeper inside. With every step I took, it was as if there were 1,000 protruding steps coming after me. The further I crept forward, the more my brain frantically signalled me to turn around and run. It was then that I heard a bang. I turned and ran away.

Harley Thomas Jeffries (15)
Dover Grammar School For Boys, Dover

Stuck

I saw people go into the woods, one per month, yet no one came out. Every now and then a rumour would spark. The rumours would be things like people seeing movement at the edge of the woods. I was curious. I wanted to see it for myself. I asked around, people refused to talk about it. All they would say was don't go into the woods. I didn't listen, I went in. Stood before me was a door. I opened it. At this point, my fate was sealed. I tried running but was pulled in. Stuck. Alone. Scared.

Toby Harrison (15)
Dover Grammar School For Boys, Dover

This Is War!

This was war. We arrived in France. The Germans were mounted on the cliffs. As we advanced, more and more men were killed. It was brutal but we pushed through. We made it to the town. Bombs were going off left, right and centre. Gunfire and screams. The ocean was red with blood. We were told this would be calm. We were smelly and dirty. We were told we could make camp in the next town but no, we were ambushed. We managed to clear them out but the worst was yet to come!

Joshua Vickers (13)
Dover Grammar School For Boys, Dover

The Haunted House

As I walked down the dark, dingy hall, the floorboards creaked and my torch flickered and went out. The hairs on my arms slowly lifted up. As I moved across the floor, I felt a spiderweb hanging from the ceiling. At the end of the hallway, I could see a room with a window. I ran to the room. As I was running, the floorboards kept creaking and crackling. In the room, I saw a dark, shadowy figure so I ran in the opposite direction and ran as fast as I could to escape...

Jayden Boumellas (13)
Dover Grammar School For Boys, Dover

Sleep

I asked it what it was. It smiled. It replied, "How have you forgotten so easily? We are you. We are the madness that lurks within you all, begging to be free at every moment in your deepest animal mind. We are what you hide from in your beds every night. We are what you sedate into silence and paralyse when you go to the nocturnal haven where we cannot tread." Those words, those damn words haunted me for my worthless, miserable existence.

Daniel William Jenkins (13)
Dover Grammar School For Boys, Dover

The Theft

I knew there would be consequences but I did it anyway. I was at the Louvre looking directly at the Mona Lisa. I was there to steal it but in the back of my mind, I was thinking, *this is a bad idea.* But I had a job to do so I put in the passcode and deactivated the lasers. It was right there in front of me. I just had to reach out and grab it. So I did. That was the worst mistake of my life. I must have forgotten a switch...

Daniel Finch (13)
Dover Grammar School For Boys, Dover

New Life

"Tell me everything you know, child," said the AI.

"All I know is my name," replied James. "I am called James."

"It looks like a memory wipe has proven successful on this occasion," stated the AI, "you may pass." James looked ahead and saw a vault door sealing an entrance. He grabbed the handle and pulled the vault door open and stepped through the opening. He looked around him and gasped, there were four huge walls towering over a field with a few scattered buildings and a small forest. It was breathtaking! James realised he had a new life.

Robin Ferizi (12)
Maidstone Grammar School, Maidstone

War's Sacrifice

"Tell me everything you know, child." Nothing. That was the sad truth.
"Let's just go," she said. "Time is of the essence." A shot of red raced past my head, I could feel the heat radiating from it. Dangerous. I followed the mysterious, abnormal woman to a barricade and readied my signature weapon - a crossbow. I shot down a couple of them, their shadowy figures collapsing and wailing. I felt awful but I had to. Another shot just avoided me, but my companion wasn't so lucky. "It's up to you now," she whispered. I knew she was right, my destiny.

Jack Calvin Doyle (12)
Maidstone Grammar School, Maidstone

The Choice

"You can save only one," the voice said from down the pitch-black tunnel. Screams filled my head, call after call, they bellowed for help. I ran and ran as fast as possible. I determined their fate. The first spine-chilling incident was my helpless mother dangling above pure peril, then I saw my friend with death next to his face, both screaming their hearts out. All I could think was, *life or death, gain or loss?* I scampered over to the split path. "So, who to choose?" whispered the voice, then my final thought was, *friend or family?*
"I choose..."

James Mylo Seaward (12)
Maidstone Grammar School, Maidstone

The Child

"Tell me everything you know, child," the tall, wiry man said.
The boy looked up and fixed the man with a stare as unbending as a lightning conductor.
"I know sir, that all life is suffering," he replied. "I know that all things will pass away and be forgotten. I know that you and I are merely shadows." The man could hold the boy's intense gaze no more and began to sob uncontrollably. He realised the boy's education was finally complete. "Why do you weep, Father?" the boy inquired.
"I weep with joy, my son. You are now a man."

Jack Kerner (12)
Maidstone Grammar School, Maidstone

The Chairman's Son

"Tell me everything you know, child," whispered the man behind the mask in a cool, calm voice. "Tell me everything and you can forget about everything that's happened."

The child began to stutter a single word. "N-n-no."

The man pulled out a small, grey pistol and placed it on the table, facing the boy. It was a Makarov Soviet semi-automatic pistol with only one purpose - to kill. The man repeated the sentence, this time with a hint of annoyance in his voice.

"Where is it?" he said while picking up the gun and pointing it at him...

Tom Hicks (12)

Maidstone Grammar School, Maidstone

Thoughtless

"You can only save one," the voice said. I gasped, speechless. A deadly silence filled the damp cage where I'd been imprisoned. My heart raced, save my family or my friend? I had no idea who these people were or what the manipulating voice was, it sounded computerised, artificial, as if not to give anything away. I could feel my blood boiling around my body, ready to bubble in anger if needed. Then, to my shock, the voice spoke again, saying how it must accept my first answer, cruelly, artificially, deathly. Thoughtless speech erupted from my mouth, killing the silence.

Samuel Woodhead (12)
Maidstone Grammar School, Maidstone

Flee

It was only me and Ben as we crept into the room that our friends were in. Suddenly, negative thoughts rushed through my head. Could we save them? Were we enough to stop the evil being that was hunting us down one by one? Fraser and Callum were okay though but I suspected not for very long.
"Help me!" cried Fraser.
"Me too!" shouted Callum. I noticed the chains wrapped around their hands but they were also hanging off the ceiling. There was an unlocking mechanism to release them. Then the stranger's voice echoed, "You can save only one."

Dominic Vaughan (12)
Maidstone Grammar School, Maidstone

A Light Breeze

My torch flickered and went out. I was now in complete and utter darkness. Before I was petrified, now I was on the verge of fainting! I was telling myself everything was going to be alright but my palms and forehead were still streaming with sweat as I knew there was someone or something else not too far away. Something vindictive, something sly, something capable of destruction but at first glance, wants peace. Suddenly, I heard three consecutive chimes. I then felt a breeze on my left shoulder. I turned swiftly around and there it was, standing right there, smiling...

Harry Trimmer (12)
Maidstone Grammar School, Maidstone

The Basement

"Tell me everything you know, child!" In a shadowy and murky basement, there were two people, a child who was small, terrified and blonde-haired, the man, on the other hand, was tall, dark-haired and cold-hearted. The boy ran to the door. It was locked so he searched and searched everywhere until he saw a dog. Luckily enough, the dog was obedient and gave him the key to the door. Suddenly, the tall, dark man stopped the boy. *Why? Why? Why?* thought the man, *why would he want to leave me in this place?* "What a stupid little boy!"

Henry Whitehead (12)
Maidstone Grammar School, Maidstone

My Last Breath

I looked around, desperately searching for an escape, my ears deafened by the constant lashing of claws and thundering growls. If one sharp dark eye landed on me, my life would be in his jaws in seconds. Fire came infinitely gushing out the spiralling stairs, leading straight towards my dungeon room. Panicking and trembling, I tried to open the door but it was locked. I almost smelt death. Rocks came crashing down from my ceiling as a huge, fierce monster with huge fangs and razor-sharp claws came. The key was strapped to his waist! There was nowhere to hide.

Jacob Carlton (12)
Maidstone Grammar School, Maidstone

Free Hostage

"You can save only one," the voice said. I was scared! He looked through his binoculars. I looked for an escape but the hill was steep. I was bound to make a noise. I stepped back and felt a jagged rock. Looking down, I picked it up. Suddenly, a click. "I wouldn't do that," he laughed. I gulped and dropped the rock. He turned to me and sighed. "Sweetie, you've got twenty minutes. If you're not back by then, your village goes boom! As well as you." Tears welled in my eyes, he raised his gun to shoot me. "Go!"

Jack Crabb (12)
Maidstone Grammar School, Maidstone

The Mysterious Dagger-Man

"Tell me all you know, child."
"I only saw a man in black with his hood up. He had a dagger pierced through his hand and he went along that alleyway. It was pitch-black so I didn't see much."
Bang! A man strolling down the alleyway dropped dead. The detective spun on his heels. A man in black, with a dagger through his hand, stood dead ahead. The murderer concealed his gun in his pocket with a spin. He drew his long, bloody sword from its sheath and plunged it into the boy's chest. Blood oozed from his body.

Ali Shelley (12)
Maidstone Grammar School, Maidstone

The Resurrection

My torch flickered and went out. I was in total darkness. However, the old, oaken branch I was holding was still sizzling strongly from the strength of the fire. I didn't notice this for a while, I could only focus on the altar, the path and the gem that I had glimpsed when the torch was bright. The altar was made of crumbling, Aztec-looking stones. The only thing keeping them together was the vines around the room. I rushed along the five-metre path, towards the dazzling scarlet gem, only anticipating its power to resurrect my love, Lucy.

Angus McPhee (12)
Maidstone Grammar School, Maidstone

Run!

I looked around, desperately searching for an escape route from the small dungeon in the cellar of the castle. It was rapidly filling with water from the dark, foreboding well in the centre of the room. I ran around the dingy, square room, the water now at my ankles, pushing every slime-covered stone. I was trying to find the secret exit the castle guard had walked out of. Eventually, when the icy cold water reached my waist, a huge slab of stone pulled over with a grinding noise. The water splashed out, I checked for the guards, then ran.

Finley Fleming (12)
Maidstone Grammar School, Maidstone

Zombie Chamber

"You can save only one," the voice said as the car departed the station. It was the ride operator, although the ride concept made me nervous because it turned each rider into a zombie! The riders were sent into the dark chamber where *it* lurked. Rusty, sharp needles tucked neatly into the rider's seat injected them with a liquid and then sharp attachments swung down and attacked the insides of their bodies. A lot of screams happened on the inside. There was no escape, except for the end of the ride, await your fall.

Charlie Broderick (12)
Maidstone Grammar School, Maidstone

The Mission

"Tell me everything you know, child," said the voice. Jack remained silent, stunned by the situation he was in. Meanwhile, the man left the room, angered by the boy refusing to say anything. Jack sat in the mysterious, dark room silently, not daring to say a word or move. The man returned to Jack, accompanied by two muscly men in matching uniforms. Together, they were able to heave Jack up off the chair, as he refused to stand up, and hauled him away. Jack was worried, he didn't know where he was going to end up...

Fergus Lennon (12)
Maidstone Grammar School, Maidstone

Desperate Escape

I looked around, desperately searching for an escape. The mountain started to rumble and shake around as rocks started to cave in on me inside of this never-ending chasm. I remembered the torch in my pocket that I could use to find an exit. Time was running out. Just in front of me, a small gap appeared so I ran for it. That was when the floor cracked, split and fell, forcing everything down with it. My instincts kicked in, forcing me to run faster, the floor catching up with me quickly. I slipped and fell rapidly, deeper. Game over.

Richard Simmonds (12)

Maidstone Grammar School, Maidstone

The Invasion

My torch flickers and goes out. I'm sure there were headlights behind me but now it's all total darkness. There is a strange scent in the air. What could it be? All of a sudden, a circle of light appears above my head. A blue beam comes down, then darkness once more. I hear a strange language like I've never heard before. I look up. Three strange creatures just stand there, staring at me. They inject a strange substance. The next thing I know, I'm back next to my car, torch working, and the other car stops to help.

Mathew Parkhouse
Maidstone Grammar School, Maidstone

The Problem At Sea

I got a call at 2am to three people's boat sinking in the middle of the Pacific Ocean. We got into our helicopter, which was low on fuel, and made our way towards the sinking boat. As it was night, we had to put on our searchlight to find the sinking boat. As we got closer to the boat we started to hear three different voices shouting.
"Help! Help!" they called at the top of their voices. When the voices got really loud, we knew that we were there.
"You can save only one," the voice beside me said...

Reece Collins (12)
Maidstone Grammar School, Maidstone

Closer...

My torch flickered and went out, the rusted door refused to open. The wind grew stronger, wanting nothing but to kill me. I'd have to rush to the side door. The tornado came closer, pulling me in like a black hole. The wind threw the wooden plank resting beside me at my face. I was a dead man. I pounded on the main door, the tornado was getting too close. I looked at the scaffolding going to another entrance. I walked over ever so carefully. It was unfinished. I felt the tornado's breath on me. I'd have to jump...

Joshua Stratulat (12)
Maidstone Grammar School, Maidstone

The Midnight Abduction

"You can save only one," the voice said. The beginning of my madness was the beginning of someone's end. My weariness was settling in as the dimly-lit country road came to an end. Oh, what had I done to deserve this? I must've taken a wrong turning ten minutes back. I had no option but to turn around, that was when it hit me, literally. I was slammed into my steering wheel, too fast for the airbag to work. As I came to, my body felt immobilised. I stared at the image dangling above. That face, once again...

Jude Wilson (12)
Maidstone Grammar School, Maidstone

Behind You

Don't go into the woods, they told me. Something is here I'm not alone. I can feel it. My heart is beating faster by the second. I need to get out of here, now! My legs are giving out on me, am I going mad? This is unusual, something moves. I'm hiding behind a tree. I peek around it to look out for any threats. *Roar!* "Oh no," I say to myself, "this is really bad!" Sticks and branches snap all around. Something touches me. I swing around with the need of light. I turn around...

Robert Andrei Mihai (12)
Maidstone Grammar School, Maidstone

The Witch

My torch flickered and went out, I was alone in the darkness. I had stumbled across the shack quite by chance, having been in the woods on the way back from my friend's new house when I saw it. I couldn't help but investigate. In the half-light, I suddenly bumped into something. I felt sick when I saw what it was - a cauldron! I backed away. Out of the gloom, a hand grabbed me, I was pushed into the cauldron. The last thing I saw before a burning match was an old woman cackling and glaring down at me...

Will Rickman (12)
Maidstone Grammar School, Maidstone

The Beast

My torch flickered and went out. Shadows seemed to be creeping out at me, feasting on my fear. Walking, walking, walking, not knowing how to escape from the dreaded beast. Suddenly, a light flickered on, a face with a twisted snarl greeted me, then I fainted.
I woke up with a bitter taste in my mouth. Blood. I was sitting on a chair, my hands were tied uncomfortably behind my back. I was in a minute room, lit by flickering lights. Then I saw it. A shadow. A twisted face. Horrific pain. Darkness.

Benjamin Walls (12)
Maidstone Grammar School, Maidstone

Save One

I woke up, my head ached and I couldn't move. As I looked around, I spotted two very familiar people, my parents! I could see they were in some sort of contraption like me. Suddenly, there was a voice. "Your parents are in a very deadly trap. When the timer runs out they will fall into a tank of acid, or you can choose to pull a rope and connect it to the metal box behind you. However, when you pull the rope of one, the other falls into the same tank of acid. You have one life to save."

Alex Liptrot (12)
Maidstone Grammar School, Maidstone

Trapped

"Tell me everything you know, child!" The hairs on my neck pricked up. I heard the corrupt breathing of a man. It was next to my ear, it felt warm like a radiator in a cold room. I was only able to see brisk movements of the other person as the room was shrouded in darkness. All of a sudden, the room burst into light. I could see the old man, he was on the other side of the room facing the other way, looking out a dirty window. In the next instant, he was stood in front of me...

Oliver Surgison (12)
Maidstone Grammar School, Maidstone

I Know You

You do not know me and you never will. I am that one with deception and mystery. I am the one who is above you yet beneath you at the same time. I am your enemy but your ally. I see you but you do not see me. I am the light to the darkness but the darkness to the light. I am all-seeing and all-knowing of the unknown but I am unaware of the future. I am that chair, that table, the person sitting next to you, I'm nothing, I am everything.

Harry Harper (12)
Maidstone Grammar School, Maidstone

The Desolate Troupe

Masking him was a shrouding aura that reeked of insanity, melancholy and hysteria. The master's scarlet eyes beckoning, commanding, forcing my sanity to abandon me. His slender figure towered over me, his presence alone shook me from within, rattling my heart like a broken instrument. Snarling, the scarlet fire grew with malice and disturbed the candles surrounding us. The troupe paraded, jeered and strangely entertained, swallowing fires, beheading each other, grinning fearlessly. Maleficent shadows danced hysterically in the light, twisting with sickening crunches that echoed in my mind. Stumbling, mumbling, I struggled outside but only darkness thrived there. Desolation.

Alban Merit (15)
Newman Catholic College, Brent

The Button

Heavy breathing plagued the air with anxiety, dread. All around, the crimson red lights danced upon my skin, etching itself into my flesh, sweat profusing from my pores. Despair. I heard the screams echoing within my mind. A fabrication. Nevertheless, I'd subconsciously sealed my ears, expecting it to stop. It didn't. The monitors mocked me, repeating the warning message over and over, mocking my humanity, mocking my sympathy, mocking my being. Telling me to give it all up, to press it. "I was coerced!" I'd say. "Forced!" I'd plead. All in vain, useless, fruitless, with the red button now pressed...

Lucas Barbosa (15)

Newman Catholic College, Brent

Limbo

This can't be happening. It is! The last time I saw her the sky was stained crimson. Blots of cream slowly passing above, a ball of flames descending as the carpet of void engulfed our world. Then it all went blank. Her soft smile shifted, crystal eyes shattering. *Don't go.* Synchronised with sundown, her figure slowly vanished behind the walls of stone. Rivulets of water collapsed one by one, crashing into her pale skin, washing away her colour, diluting her soul. I tightened my grip around my fate. *Weakling.* At least I'd see her again. *Don't.* I smiled. *Idiot.* Trigger.

Hasan Al-timimi (14)

Newman Catholic College, Brent

The Haze

Frozen, terrified, conscious. Her world spinning, her life crashing faster than comprehensible, a red, majestic dance unleashed before her hollow eyes, leaving her soul scarred. This was new, her senses awoke. As soon as she realised there was no time for goodbyes, no time for sorrow, she knew forgiveness was obsolete, not only for them but herself as well. Her mum's unearthly figure was there, smiling, but Emma's eyes were blinded by the boundaries reality imposed upon her. *I can't give up now,* she thought. This was irreversible, dangerous, but she was willing to fight. The games had just begun...

Mihai Munteanu (15)
Newman Catholic College, Brent

Technocracy Armageddon

Boom! The explosion had the brawn of a meteor, causing clouds of deceased preys to disperse in all directions. From high above, the darkness unfurled like a disease and obscured the land, eliminating any hope that resided within the miasma. The scorched, battle-damaged vehicles lined up elegantly beside the street while an unidentified object stood firmly in the distance. The air, land and environment recklessly fought for the vestige in a phantasmagoria of destruction; the ashes of a world-ending crisis. The living and the dead would reunite at this one moment. The moment that ended all life on this planet.

Nimeire Sala Mavounda Junior (14)
Newman Catholic College, Brent

Civil War

Science has vastly improved and so has mechanical engineering in these past few years. Bio-mechanical engineers have been able to accomplish their most desired goal after continuous attempts. They were able to successfully implant a stable human brain into a machine, an AI, gifting them with supposed human emotion and imagination, allocating them on the same level as humans, if not higher. They named it ZS295, the prototype. Soon after this event, a middle-aged man had been arrested (perhaps wrongfully) for protesting and rebelling against sector 3, the non-democratic government. His name was Jack Smith. Injustice!

Brandon Gouveia (14)
Newman Catholic College, Brent

Enclosure

My teeth clamped together, each disfigured building-like tooth moulding together. Occasionally, my clamp-like mouth opened, triggering repeated spasms where my teeth collided, each time scraping my teeth little by little into futile dust, slowly diffusing into the multitudes of mixtures that accompanied us, air. Eyes flickered as if a child played with them. Drowsy, I tried to avoid the inevitable. Each blink was a struggle, as if glue was deposited along the lining of my eye, amplifying and strengthening each. Finally, I dozed off into my subconscious. The empty nothingness we face at the end of each day - sleep.

Joshua Gomes (14)
Newman Catholic College, Brent

The Chase

The darkness lingered as the distressed boy ran from building to building, in an attempt to outpace his pursuers. As the charcoal-enriched environment surrounded the troubled orphan, even though quadcopters scanned the scene, he was able to escape the copter's vision. Although the child's location was explicit to the quadcopter's thermal sensors, he evaded the ground of rogue chasers without a trace. The central government labelled rogues as a disease, a glitch in a programme. He spent his life running but he never looked back to see what he'd left behind. He wanted a normal life, he had to fight.

Aman Alemayehu (14)
Newman Catholic College, Brent

Forest

What an exquisite sight, filling it in with oak trees, with numerous sticks and several leaves. Ultramarine blue with a quick sight of maroon spots. Blood. Thoroughly, the air became visible, erasing the view with its wrath. Lifting my foot from one to another, precisely not slaying another creature, a rambunctious bird stuck next to me - bullet in its heart. Someone was there, following me, hearing my swift, intense heartbeat and my lightened steps. Gunshots. Bullets rushed past me. Glancing over my shoulder, a black silhouette appeared. My steps quickened and I heard another. I descended into the lake, alone.

Simeon Bozhilov (14)
Newman Catholic College, Brent

Who, What, When, Where And How?

You float in the endless time, darkness and abyss. All you can visualise is coal-black around you, making your senses confused. You wonder to yourself, asking countless times, *where am I?* You're floating like a feather but never in contact with an object. Your brain starts to question, *where are we?* Still a light feather, you then realise that you're being consumed! You're withering away in the depths of darkness, slowly feeling agony and camouflaging in the deep, dark dungeon. You're being consumed by darkness as your whole body now asks, *where in this world are we?*

Lemar Whyte (14)
Newman Catholic College, Brent

Abnormal

I looked around, desperately searching for an escape. Vivid lights were flickering, revealing the painted blood dripping from the walls, crawling towards me steadily. The rotten plank of wood screamed as it shattered into small pieces, causing my blood to boil as the creature stood there, staring at me with fury in its golden, grey, emotionless eyes. Everything went silent, the only thing I could hear was my tiny, innocent heart beating vigorously, causing my chest to tense, gasping for air as I breathed heavily. And then everything slowly turned dark, fading away, causing me to enter my dream state.

Daniel Liszkovics (15)
Newman Catholic College, Brent

Ancient Times

With a slicing slash from the ancient, razor-sharp sword, the innocent died. The heat ball (raging sunlight) astonishingly spectated the monstrous, crippled human, engulfing a ferocious life to save his life. There was a half-naked human wearing an ugly green skirt like Tarzan, his reckless body all covered with shocking scars, his one eye covered with black cloth like a ferocious, funny-looking pirate. His nasty words of venom, his long legs like an athlete springing towards a second same-looking creature. Gradually, they started fighting vigorously, punching and pushing, just for worthless money.

Keniel Augusto Vales (14)
Newman Catholic College, Brent

The Sun And Moon

The ball rolled silently throughout the soundless hollow, shadowing the world until total darkness. The lantern of hope shined goodness for those who wished for it. Darkness frightened their soul, foretold to be day and night. Day, to be seen holy and sacred. Night, to hide our sorrows in its mists, for night is where we're in our deepest state: sorrow, guilt, regret. These emotions fun, flaunting themselves. We are two-faced with the mischievous thoughts that we neither portray nor tell. Love is what we are numb to but hate, what we're showered in. Like a coin we flip continuously.

Aleksander Jaranowski (14)
Newman Catholic College, Brent

Artificial Anger

Nathan created something dangerous, something he couldn't control, that could lead to the end of this crumbling empire. He never wished for this. The whole time, he wanted to solidify this dying nation. Soon, there would be nothing to save. His monster-like creation had access to all weapons and the monster was driven by anger towards the government. He could end it all. The key to stopping this threat was wrapped around Nathan's arm. The radiating green rubber jackets, the metallic box that held the monster's real memory. Nathan wished for this to be over. There was one way...

Arvie Nicolas (14)
Newman Catholic College, Brent

Erehania

"It's really not that hard looking for your pet phoenix in Antarctica," I told myself over and over again until the feeling reverberated in a cacophony of reassurance, my hope wearing away into evanescing darkness just as the little warmth inhabited my stomach. The butterflies evolved into pterodactyls that gnawed at my shivering intestines. How had this started? Good question. Twenty-four hours ago, the mailman told me that my father was the greatest sorcerer that ever lived and I was heir to the throne of a forgotten land called Erehania. You know, the usual, no biggie!

Adil Bogere (14)
Newman Catholic College, Brent

End

The future is here, pale, white armour hiding a technological terror with a keen mission of ending civilisation. A face of inarticulate expressions providing more fear to all who are unfortunate to see its metallic armour of vibrant titanium. Stiff arms with fast, unpredictable movements. Only two hours ago, the strongest army base proved to be weak, technology beyond any human mind. Nothing can be done to stop this extraterrestrial robot and only time will tell what is yet to happen. Fear is evenly scattered around the globe as humans have nowhere to run in this weak planet of ours.

Caio Veroneze (14)
Newman Catholic College, Brent

History Of The Forresters

The battle was tied. Our forces were great fighters from Ugo and Forrester factions. The defenders of the fort were also great, blasting mercenaries from the renowned Bolton faction. The clashing of swords was deafening, combined with the screams of another man being butchered by an iron sword. Occasionally, a volley of arrows would be fired, creating a harmony of whistles as they flew past. But then, a very unpleasant sound interrupted the mix. A loud war horn was played, all the Forrester soldiers knew what this meant. They turned their heads and saw the Ugo retreating. Traitors.

Ozzy Majewski (14)
Newman Catholic College, Brent

The Miracle Escape

I looked around, desperately searching for an escape but I couldn't see anything. All around me was trees, huge trees. The air was foggy. I started getting more desperate. I thought to myself, *that's it, there's no way of getting out of here*. However, suddenly, a bright light illuminated between the trees. When I saw the light, I believed it could be a path, a way out of the terrible forest. I started following the light. After thirty minutes, I was exhausted after running. I had to find anything to drink so I could get hydrated and continue my journey...

Julio Cesar Dias Neto (15)
Newman Catholic College, Brent

The Forest

Don't go into the woods, they told me as I strode in arrogantly and stupidly. There was nothing particularly special or mystical about the forest, or so I thought. As I inhaled, the horrific, deadly scent of rotting, toxic mushrooms intoxicated my nostrils like a needle penetrating my vulnerable skin with such ease. There I stood, pitifully gasping for fresh air like a hopeless dog drowning because of its idiotic actions. Gasping for air, I heard a deafening rustle in the looming bushes. I stepped back nervously like prey frozen in terror in front of its undisputed predator.

Aerhon Espiritu Abante (15)
Newman Catholic College, Brent

Plane Crash

"You can only save one," the voice spoke in a harsh manner. I've never been so torn between two sides. It was like choosing between Hell or Heaven, the feeling was indescribable. Four days before, the plane crashed. As I crawled to the airport, I was awfully tired, same as Timmy and Helen. Making sure that we hadn't forgotten our belongings or documentation, not knowing in a few days it would be pure survival and none of this would even matter, we went towards the plane. I saw thunder strike above. Timmy asked, "Is everything going to be okay?"

Daniel Gladkins (16)
Newman Catholic College, Brent

The Man Who Killed Earth

Kobi Lee, now twenty, survived an explosion. Unfortunately, it killed his family, friends and everyone. Every day, regret purged him. Why did he do it? Kobi Lee led a life of despair, he thought the explosion would solve everything. It didn't. Kobi Lee thought genocide was the way to cleanse the human race. There was nothing else in the world but Kobi Lee. The elements themselves exploded into disappearance. Water evaporated, fire stopped burning, the sky fell, the wind faded, the sun went cold and forgot interest in man. What was left? Nothing. Kobi Lee, now twenty, dead.

Gavin Bond (14)
Newman Catholic College, Brent

Void

Destruction dominated the scarce hope. The sunlight withered across the horizon as darkness approached the sky's gradient. Citizens were drenched in a cloak of melancholy as they looked back at their fallen city for the last time. A grey mass cloaked the execution of the once monotonous city, balloons of smoke rose up into the air, encapsulating the city in a dark void. The artificial intelligence left the city in a scare. The fragments of cement tilted in the echoes of grief, with no particular pattern. Angela stood in severe perplexity, the city she once knew was gone.

Tre Holmes (14)
Newman Catholic College, Brent

The Light

Flashing, gloomy lights pierced through the emerald surface of the tinted windows. My ghost haunted me as it smothered the crooked wall behind me. Every inch I shuffled was mimicked by this black, luminous figure. The ice-cold diffused into my body and turned me static as flakes dropped like water droplets out of my nose. The door creaked open with a little tweak noise constantly repeating into my head as the drumming sound of the man's footsteps zoomed closer. The shadows above isolated me in the corner as it engulfed my vision. There he was, his head slowly emerged...

Farid Fayez (15)

Newman Catholic College, Brent

The Mysterious World Of Battleground

I opened up my parachute, ready to drop on the balcony on the house. I had a sort of clock that always kept me connected with my friend, Everest. We were both dropping at the same area and were always talking about what was happening.
Finally, when I landed, I saw some weapons, first aid kits, armour and grenades. "I'm assuming that we have to fight," I said to Everest.
"Probably."
I took everything I could and ended up with a shotgun and an M16. Instead, Everest had a sniper and an AKM.
"Okay, now we can win this."

Denis Popa (15)
Newman Catholic College, Brent

United We Stand

As we three fell apart from each other, regretting every move we took, we fell into that nasty diversion of the sacrificial pawn played by the head AI, Maria. As they don't have genders, we nickname them by their behaviours. The team was practised for dealing with situations like this, being separated from each other. We were placed in a torture chamber for twenty-four hours. This took place once a week with different traps. Although situations like these weren't life-threatening, we grew up training in worse situations, fighting for each other's lives.

Franklin Rodrigues (14)
Newman Catholic College, Brent

Cold Steel

Please let this be a dream, I thought as I plummeted uncontrollably off the edge and into the trail, swimming in suffocating pelts of silvery-grey fur. My hand wrestled through and clasped the oak-finished handle of the shotgun. I hoisted myself off the floor, only to be swept back down, gazing at the unconcealed moon. Running out of patience, I fired two shells, one after the other, into the rows of trees. Murderous eyes stabbed into my person. Within an instant, I was ripped apart by saliva-coated fangs. I became a bloody mess, losing my consciousness.

Niruzan Thangeswaran (15)
Newman Catholic College, Brent

Yellow Lights Hurt Our Eyes

The dusk of dawn had just broken out, it was better safe in here. Thinking about it now, I wouldn't be able to imagine what it was like anymore. How many of them were there? How long would it take for things to be normal? Years? Decades? Counting the stacks on the shelf, a large portion was still available, luckily. Looking back at my horrendous image in the mirror, what exactly was the norm anymore? The reflection in the mirror displayed... a human! Scruffy, an overwhelming amount of hair, bloodshot crimson eyes and jagged, stained teeth. *Who am I?*

Eric Nunes-Elias (15)
Newman Catholic College, Brent

Mythos

Cane dashed towards Abel. Cane assassinated Abel with a rusty rock. As Abel fell - his crimson blood conquered the world. Cane was then banished to the land of Nod, where he formed a faction called The Brotherhood of Nod. After taking down his brother, Cane got cursed due to Abel's holy blood falling on Cane's forehead. The curse caused Cane to become eternal; this meant that Cane would now be able to betray his Stygian master. Due to his immortality, Cane would now never age. Cane would use this power to avenge his brother Abel. Abel lived in death...

Syed Ali Raza (15)
Newman Catholic College, Brent

Forgiveness

A long time ago in a far land called Metro City, lived a young boy called Metroman. He was sent from Saturn. One day, Metroman went home to find his family dead. He buried them the next day and afterwards, he felt like he needed to catch this foul criminal. He said, "Whoever did this unspeakable crime shall bear no mercy with my hands!" He later had his friend arrested after finding out that George had deceived him. George begged for forgiveness but Metroman couldn't forgive George for the unfaithful, foul crimes he'd committed.

Luke Pitter (13)
Newman Catholic College, Brent

The Beginning Of The End

As the dim speck of light faded away, a bang emerged from nothing. The electrifying taser of the sub-atomic alarmed, unleashing planets and creatures. The universe was created. While life seemed to strive, life also seemed to fade. The rapid decrease and increase of creatures mesmerised Michael. He'd heard stories of how the universe had begun from nothing but now he could only imagine how it could all go back to being nothing again. Michael was young, only twenty years old. However, his village had a decline in resources and everyone started dying...

Elvis Buchan (14)
Newman Catholic College, Brent

Race To The End

The fate of all humanity was decided when pen was put to paper. Every news outlet in the world had talked about the signing of the *commission act*... The foul odour of poisonous gas, however dangerous, was the only thing keeping me alive. The smoke emitting from the bombs thrown were leading me to the exit of the crumbling building. The urge of getting to safety, the dreaded gas and the sweat flooding from my head was pushing me closer and closer to the edge. The world unravelled right in front of my eyes; illusions and hallucinations took over.

Emmanuel Jeremiah Abebe (14)
Newman Catholic College, Brent

The Darkest Minds Conceive The Brightest Dreams

Since the first trickle of water hit a human's throat, there has been the desire to act evil, despite absolution and realism. But how many of these so-called villains of society were actually villains? Although the way they have used their plan could be seen as evil, inhuman and demonic, their overall ideas were brilliant. Some might go as far to call them geniuses! But we refuse to acknowledge the good in their evil and instead label them as Hitlers of the world. However, I won't make the same mistake my father did. I will cure humanity.

Amarion Thompson (15)
Newman Catholic College, Brent

It's Coming Home

It was nightfall but something in particular felt imperfect. I was agitated and unnerved. There was a whisper in the back. I methodically turned around to witness something which unearthed me. It was him. He looked at me with a quick smirk in his tangy, orange-like suit. He planted something into the ground and left without a trace. I rapidly ran down the stairs, trying not to alert my mum from her slumber. I opened the door to see a sudden glow outside shining a bright indigo. At that point in time, I was prepared to acquire my complex mission.

Donte Tabios (14)
Newman Catholic College, Brent

Swine Trouble

In a world where pigs ruled, being able to stand on two feet and where pigs flew, Haven, a normal citizen of Swine World, one day wandered off to find what appeared to be a path with a trail of food. Haven's brain told him to follow and eat the food, while his consciousness told him to follow the path and respectfully leave the food alone. As he followed the trail, suddenly, *slam!* He hit a lamp post so he stopped eating and continued, unexpectedly finding what appeared to be a vortex leading to another world that looked like his...

Pedro Vieira (13)

Newman Catholic College, Brent

Fight Between Two Mafias

Andre came in front of Joshua's car and suddenly, Joshua pressed his car brakes so hard that even the tyres made noise. It was Andre's Mafia members that were chasing Joshua. As Andre was just in the middle of the road, Joshua got out of the car and helped Andre to get to the side of the road. Suddenly, Andre's friends appeared. While they were running towards Joshua, he got to his car and drove towards the countryside, where his gang lived.
As he got there, Andre's gang knew where they lived so they planned to go later...

Imtishal Choudhry (15)
Newman Catholic College, Brent

Prevail

Today, my worst nightmares came to light. It was a miserable night and my dad, mother and two brothers had all disappeared from our sinister house to visit my grandma. I was alone. Anxiously glaring into the abyss-like depths of the room, I consciously pleaded that nothing was there. Glaring back at me, I felt its satanic presence, which had abused me for as long as I could remember, cramming the room with its lack of remorse, greed, jealousy and lust. I was no longer there, I was no longer me. Darkness maliciously engulfed me, prevailing.

Lemar Francis (15)
Newman Catholic College, Brent

Secrets That Lie Within

In the glorious, magnificent city of Blackpool, England, there lived a drunken and violent man named Liam Parker. Liam grew up as an alcoholic and was arrested twice as a fourteen-year-old for assault with a firearm and breaking and entering an elderly person's house. Liam was a forklift driver for a Blackpool construction company. Liam had to lie his way into the company without revealing his troubling past to them. He was attempting to leave and head to the pub when he was suddenly knocked out by a group of unknown assailants...

Elias Yabiib (14)
Newman Catholic College, Brent

At The Forest Night

In the forest, I heard a noise. I didn't know what had happened but I was terrified. I thought Jack left the door unlocked. Jack was my best friend, he came over for two days. I was sleeping before the noise, it sounded like someone was downstairs but it could've been an animal or a ghost. I went back to bed.
After ten minutes, another noise. I heard someone screaming for help. I woke Jack up to see what was going on. We went downstairs. I couldn't believe what I saw! I felt something behind me so I turned around...

Pedro Peixoto (14)
Newman Catholic College, Brent

Snow Siege

"You can only save one," the voice said. I felt a cold hand grasp my shoulder and throw me viciously to the floor while simultaneously getting kicked behind my knee, indicating to go on my knees. I complied instantly, hoping it would give me an insight to my situation. The sound of the crushed snow echoed through the forest like a bullet slicing the air. I adjusted my eyes to halfway. The sun glared down and penetrated my eyes like a woodpecker pecking a tree.
"I'll decide then." *Click, click!*

Lemarr Moffatt (15)
Newman Catholic College, Brent

The Cliff

The heaviness of the air made it hard to breathe. Lungs filled with the icy air of the night, shivering legs rooted into the cliffside; my life on the edge of the knife. Strands of grass cut into my feet. The dark sea opened towards the heavens. Bubbling water climbed up the cliff, the ground slipped underneath my feet; my pulse thin. At the point of no return, his hungry hands pushed against my fragile back. Suddenly, the blissful ocean opened its hands. The distance was closing as my eyelids hugged. My feet let go, gone forever.

Vladut Iacob (15)

Newman Catholic College, Brent

Checking Out My History!

I was walking through the chartered and stretching streets. I looked around, desperately searching for an escape. I heard a powerful voice. "Don't go in the woods, we will find you!" they told me. This led me to a deep impression of no hope, no dreams, no future. Running rapidly through the trees, which were also my guardians, I put all my hope in them. I was looking for my history, my identity, but I never found it. I could hear how the people were following me. There was no escape but I put all my hope into nature.

Ricardo Vasalie (15)
Newman Catholic College, Brent

Room 72

Huff, puff, huff. I paced down the rocky pavement, hoping that some miraculous event would happen, maybe waking up and realising it was just a dream. The noise of the thuds of the thing behind was getting closer and closer by the second. It was catching up and I was getting exhausted. I tried to angle my ears to see if I heard the exact location of where they were. However, I was too tired. I felt an electric shock go through my body and then darkness.

I reopened my eyes to see the number 72 carved into the door...

Helder Pinto (14)
Newman Catholic College, Brent

Shops

The boy was stranded on an island. He heard his mum shouting to him. He went through the dreaded door in the room. He walked through the aisle and saw his mum in a fuming mood. She told the boy to go to the shops. He was cautious with his words when he spoke with the immense shopkeeper. His grubby fingers twitching, the muck in his nail disturbed the boy. He shoved the money to the shopkeeper, the coin spun in circles. They both stared, realising they were wasting time. The boy panted. He knocked and waited, he was frustrated...

Reuben Francisco Soares (14)
Newman Catholic College, Brent

End Of Us

It was another day in this world of misery where hatred was spread. The weather was dull. I went to the park, hoping something would change, but it got worse. The trees slowly fell apart, people fought. When someone died, a leaf fell from a tree with the victim's name on it.
On my way home, I heard that another country had gone underwater. No survivors. I carried on walking. All of a sudden, my legs didn't want to move! My arms stuck to my body, my eyes struggled to stay open. Another leaf fell with my name on it.

Abraham Alvarez Ponte (14)
Newman Catholic College, Brent

The Broken Man

She's looking as angelic as ever, her glossy white dress mirrors the brightness of her personality. Her dedication to work and her superpower to pounce over any obstacle is the reason I'm not ceasing to exist. And now she's dead. All I ever lived for, all I ever fought for is currently in my arms covered in an ocean of blood. My paper-white shirt is now blood-red. All the guns pointing at me, with no more meaning in this cruel world, I murder until absolutely nothing is alive, except for me and my everlasting love.

Ali Mohamed (14)
Newman Catholic College, Brent

Premeditated Murder

Lifeless. A brutal murder with a skull crushed, bathing in their own blood, rotting away every second of the day. Time was being taken away again and the bloodthirsty psycho was loose in the city, shortening the time people had to live. I had to wait for them to slip up and seize the moment quickly so I could put this demon back in Hell. A brown leather wallet with two drops of blood on it was on the bathroom floor where the victim's finger pointed. I opened the wallet. Their license said 'Matthew Mike Myer's'.

Isaiah Yisrael (14)
Newman Catholic College, Brent

You And I

It was much better facing the sea, the reflection of me and you. Remember those days when we held hands hiding from our parents, hiding behind the hay? Remember those days when we thought that our love would last forevermore? You, my dolce amore, we dreamt that we would have five children. Remember those days? When your hands were running through my hair, your soul pierced into mine. Remember the days when you damaged my heart, when you left me in the hay with my brother beside you? You left me with tears. Why is it always me?

Kurt Hans Almirez (14)
Newman Catholic College, Brent

Dark Empire

Don't go in the woods, they told me that day. I was young, frightened and childish. But not anymore! I was ready, ready to know the truth about that dark, mysterious and chastened forest. I had to find him. I would have passed through the dark, fought the scariest creatures to bring him home. My brother disappeared in ninety-eight so I decided to go into the woods. The sun was completely buried in the trees, which covered the sky. No animals. No signs of life. Nothing. Now I was starting to tremble. Now I started to know.

Everest Ceka (15)
Newman Catholic College, Brent

Survival

My eyes opened, I felt terrified about what was going to happen. I was strapped into a wheelchair and transferred to room 101 until further notice.
The clock was ticking and minutes passed until a man in a white lab coat and black rubber gloves came to the room to knock me out cold.
My eyes opened and I felt the cold air rushing into my face. I realised I was falling face first, metres away from my body hitting the green, translucent spears of the grass growing out of the brown soil, shattering my bones into dust.

Matthew Smith (14)
Newman Catholic College, Brent

Alarm

Our substitute maths teacher blasted the method of the exercises and how we should all know the basics of maths. The class was all loud with laughs and screams, my stomach ached from the terrible jokes my classmates were making. I decided to put my head down and close my eyes.
Time passed and it was almost the end of the class when I woke up to the bell, not the normal bell that would indicate you to leave the classes, but a loud and obnoxious alarm that almost made me deaf. It was a lockdown, everyone was panicking...

Rafael Marques (15)
Newman Catholic College, Brent

The Mirror Of Truth

As we landed on the ground of the gods, I felt a different atmosphere. I walked towards the abandoned village. As I got closer, the mood changed. The village was in crumbs. I heard the legend about the gate and the protectors. I was searching, not giving up.
At last, I found it. It was humongous! When I got closer, three huge golems came out of the ground. They were made of rock, fire and the third one was the biggest, water. I looked at the door. I saw three spaces for stones. The three stones were the three golems.

Mark Alexa (14)
Newman Catholic College, Brent

Agent 47

Devilish danger lurked as I crept around each uncharted street, evil buttling my thoughts. Nerves racing, pressuring me, I was the target, the dead man walking. Fear suddenly came upon me, danger on the verge of finding me. Just doing as I was commanded, leading to my grace. Subconsciously, my legs swiftly tried to dare me, taking action. The number on my neck determined my fate, 47. It somehow miraculously appeared there. I had no knowledge of that world that was known as safety. Would I ever be able to get that feeling?

Romain Ebanks (15)
Newman Catholic College, Brent

The 'Thing'

The unsettling sound of leaves crunching rose, it was getting closer. Adrenaline surged through my body like venom. I gripped onto my knife as I slowly yet cautiously turned my fragile body around. I didn't know what made me do it but I closed my clammy eyes and started blindly waving my knife around like a lunatic. Maybe it was the fear of what it could do to me, maybe I was engulfed by the fact that there was no going back. I needed to face the consequences of my disastrous actions. Whatever it was, it was now over.

Prince Santos San Diego (15)
Newman Catholic College, Brent

The Saviour

The teacher said, "Give me your thumb!" Without any second thoughts, he cut his thumb and gave it to his teacher. His teacher was like Satan. When the kid cut this thumb, he didn't even feel sad or guilty, he was smiling, he was happy! He knew his mission was complete.
After a few years, there was a war, a gigantic war that was going to swallow the whole world. Everyone was in agony, everyone was sad, then a man came, only one came but he singlehandedly saved the whole world! His name was The Saviour.

Vidit Dalmia (15)
Newman Catholic College, Brent

The New World

It all started with a massive earthquake that was never seen before. Sadly, a teenage boy called Joey had to go in-between the massive crack, which actually led him out of Earth and into space. He was losing his oxygen like his life. He tried holding his breath but it was no hope. He slowly lost control of his body and closed his eyes with a teardrop. Suddenly, his eyes opened with shock and confusion. He felt like he was wearing a metal suit. His body felt stiff. He looked around the room, it was covered with robots...

Paul Sagun (14)
Newman Catholic College, Brent

The Ghost

As I stood undecided, an invisible hand seemed to sweep out the candles on the table. With a cry of terror, I dashed the bottle into the corner, then into the window. As the wind came in the house, I shivered. It felt like two bags of ice went through my spine. I was frantic with the horror of the coming darkness. The ghost zoomed in and out, my lips started to jiggle. It was like a ragged stormcloud sweeping out the stars. From candle to candle, in vain, struggling against the ambience, the ghost came to me. I died.

Daniyal Rasool (14)
Newman Catholic College, Brent

The Bully

It was a cold, gloomy, mild day. I knew from the look on his face. The violent savagery in his eyes looked straight into my soul. I knew I was his prey. As I came closer, I got more frightened. I looked around, desperately searching for an escape. He was an enormous, large beast with a rock-hard, devilish appearance. He had a baseball bat in his hand from the battle of Cain and Abel, where Cain used a club to kill his brother. I knew it was me today. My heart started pumping very fast. I tried moving backwards...

Savio Rodrigues (15)
Newman Catholic College, Brent

The Beast

It was 3am. Suddenly, I was awoken by the sound of furious knocking on my basement door. I was so frightened that I was paralysed with fear. I felt as if my life was passing by, every second felt like a century. The banging continued at a much faster rate. It then stopped. I heard loud steps coming down my stairs. I ducked under my covers. I started praying in my sobs. I was all alone. Out of curiosity, I decided to take a peek. I looked, there was a huge man, six-foot-five. He looked with a vicious smirk...

Adam Pambakian (15)
Newman Catholic College, Brent

Death Game

It is a cold and windy day in Vesperia and it is the first day of the death game. The death game is an unendurable time, we people are forced to kill. It was created to keep people in place.
I hear noises around me. *Is it here? Is somebody here? Will I die?* I think to myself. Suddenly, out of nowhere, a bullet skims the top of my head, inches from ending my suffering. There is me and him. *What do I do?* I think to myself. I turn around the tree and shoot but he's gone, somewhere...

Remarrae Jenkins (13)
Newman Catholic College, Brent

The World Of Today Has Washed Me Away

We knew each other since nursery, he was my best friend from the day we had met. It felt like his soul complemented mine and vice versa. We grew up as brothers. I was an only child so to me, he was my brother. Only, I wish I lived in the alternate universe, where that ideology was more realistic than surreal. We did everything together, then life struck us so thunderously. It sent us to war. Today I am haunted by the rusty, copper bullet that scattered his innocent blood onto my now one shade of red hands.

Lucas Bento (15)
Newman Catholic College, Brent

The Secret

No one knows this place, no one knows where I am. I am hidden, lost, alone. I sense it, sense the animal of all animals, it is hunting me, it is seeking me. I know it wants to do something involving me. I sense something. A vibration. A booming one. It is getting louder, louder than the thoughts, the thoughts in my head. It is getting quieter, quieter and quieter. I hear nothing, nothing but nature surrounding me, the winds, the fireflies. No one knows this place, no one knows where I am. No one but me.

Maksymilian Mirga (14)
Newman Catholic College, Brent

Unwanted Saga

My flight landed. Massive numbers of cars, gigantic amounts of police and militaries, in wait for me. Feeling like Hell, leaving me with goosebumps, feeling terrified, every step forward made me feel my life was in threat. Circled around me, I couldn't run away through this gigantic army. My hands handcuffed, holding my neck, they pushed me along their cars. People all over stared at me as if I was on the way to Hell. It was clear that I was heading towards the worst time of my life but I was ready.

Meriston Barbosa (15)
Newman Catholic College, Brent

The Resurrection

This all started in 1976. I was twenty-six years old. I had trained for many years and finally became a soldier. But I was no ordinary soldier. At the age of sixteen, I was taken into a lab with someone with honey, gold and some sort of dark matter. She had injected me with a lethal liquid called paracetamol. She was called Moira and it wasn't until this day that I wanted to find her and punish her for doing such evil things to me. It was after that that I finally noticed I would never be the same.

Vitor Marques (14)
Newman Catholic College, Brent

My Dream

Please let this be a dream, I thought in my mind while I prayed to God to not wake me up. I thought in my mind, *what would have happened if this was the real world?* This is the story of my dream, the dream I didn't complete. The dream that was cut in half by the hands of the terrific teachers. This is my dream that I tried to realise at school but no one helped me to do my best. This is the dream of a boy that couldn't help his friends because he didn't have the power...

Tomás Dos Santos Moniz (15)
Newman Catholic College, Brent

Different Planet

Please let this be a dream, I thought because this looked like a dream from which I couldn't wake up. I was in a different place. I saw Earth, which was particularly huge but the distance was many light years away from this planet. I didn't know what I could do because I came here from nowhere. I wanted to go back to my home, where my parents were. That was horrible for me because even I didn't know how to breathe. I didn't know how I'd get back to my parents and home.

Sebastian Dubiec (15)
Newman Catholic College, Brent

Sound

The creepy sound came from nowhere. Maybe from the east. Creation or destruction? The frightening, furious wind danced away firmly. There was a pause. Live or die? There was another pause from the west, or maybe south. I could see no one around the area, or I was blind, one or the other. Rapidly, I ran away to the north. If I looked behind, I was dead. If I looked left or right, I was dead. I was told not to go there but I did. It was a mistake. I was looking for a way to escape. I couldn't!

Marut Vijaykumar (14)
Newman Catholic College, Brent

The Cake Trap

As he strolled along the seashore, he saw a slice of fluffy, light brown sponge cake with pale white and hot pink icing. He walked towards the cake and slowly leaned over to pick it up. During that moment, a sea creature shot straight out of the water and grabbed onto him and dragged him into the water. It had aqua green, deep sea and night sky blue scales on its tail. It had long, dark blonde, wavy hair that was flowing everywhere. It was a beautiful mermaid. But good or evil?

Kameron Edwards (13)
Newman Catholic College, Brent

Escape

As I ran to the walkway, I saw two police officers coming in the same direction that I was going. I hid myself in the corner of the walkway. The police officer had an automatic weapon with a sharp knife in his right hand. He looked around everywhere but I stayed in the same place. Suddenly, the other police officer asked the officer to come and check another place. It was my luckiest day!
After the police had gone, it was my turn to run, but someone was there...

Krunil Rajendra Sauchande (14)
Newman Catholic College, Brent

Jack And Leah

It was night-time. I was heading down the street towards the shop with my girlfriend, Leah. We held hands, I had a smile on my face. Two vehicles rushed to our location. Four men rushed out of a vehicle with black ski masks on. One landed a punch in my face. My girlfriend screamed my name as they took her. The vehicle drove away. I sprinted to the vehicle as it left. A car came interrupting, knocking me out, unconscious.
I woke in a hospital.

Samuel Davis (14)
Newman Catholic College, Brent

Strange Night

Don't go in the woods, they told me but I wouldn't listen to it. It was night and I was freezing cold. Every noise in the woods was a huge thing for me. One of those noises was a truly huge thing. A huge man with a suit, a white face appeared to me. The only feeling that I could feel was that I was about to die. Then he was coming closer to me, saying that he was my friend. I just tried to run but I fell over really hard...

Deyvid De Souza Moreira (14)
Newman Catholic College, Brent

YOUNG WRITERS INFORMATION

We hope you have enjoyed reading this book – and that you will continue to in the coming years.

If you're a young writer who enjoys reading and creative writing, or the parent of an enthusiastic poet or story writer, do visit our website **www.youngwriters.co.uk**. Here you will find free competitions, workshops and games, as well as recommended reads, a poetry glossary and our blog.

If you would like to order further copies of this book, or any of our other titles, then please give us a call or visit **www.youngwriters.co.uk**.

Young Writers
Remus House
Coltsfoot Drive
Peterborough
PE2 9BF
(01733) 890066
info@youngwriters.co.uk